When Sheep Sleep

by Laura Numeroff

illustrated by David McPhail

Abrams Books for Young Readers
New York

When you can't fall asleep,
Then try counting sheep!

But what do you do if the sheep are asleep?

Count deer in the forest
Instead of the sheep.
Together all nuzzled,
They don't make a peep!

Count cows in the meadow
Instead of the sheep.
But under the moonlight,
They've fallen asleep!

Count pigs in the pig pen
Instead of the sheep.
They wiggle in mud,
And snore in a heap.

Count puppies on pillows
Instead of the sheep.
All cozy and cuddled,
They curl up to sleep.

Count birds in the treetop
Instead of the sheep.
Dreaming high in their nest,
They can't hear a cheep!

Count cats on the sofa
Instead of the sheep.
They're all purring softly,
and snuggled asleep.

Count bears in the cave den
Instead of the sheep.
Their mom watches closely,
Their safety to keep.

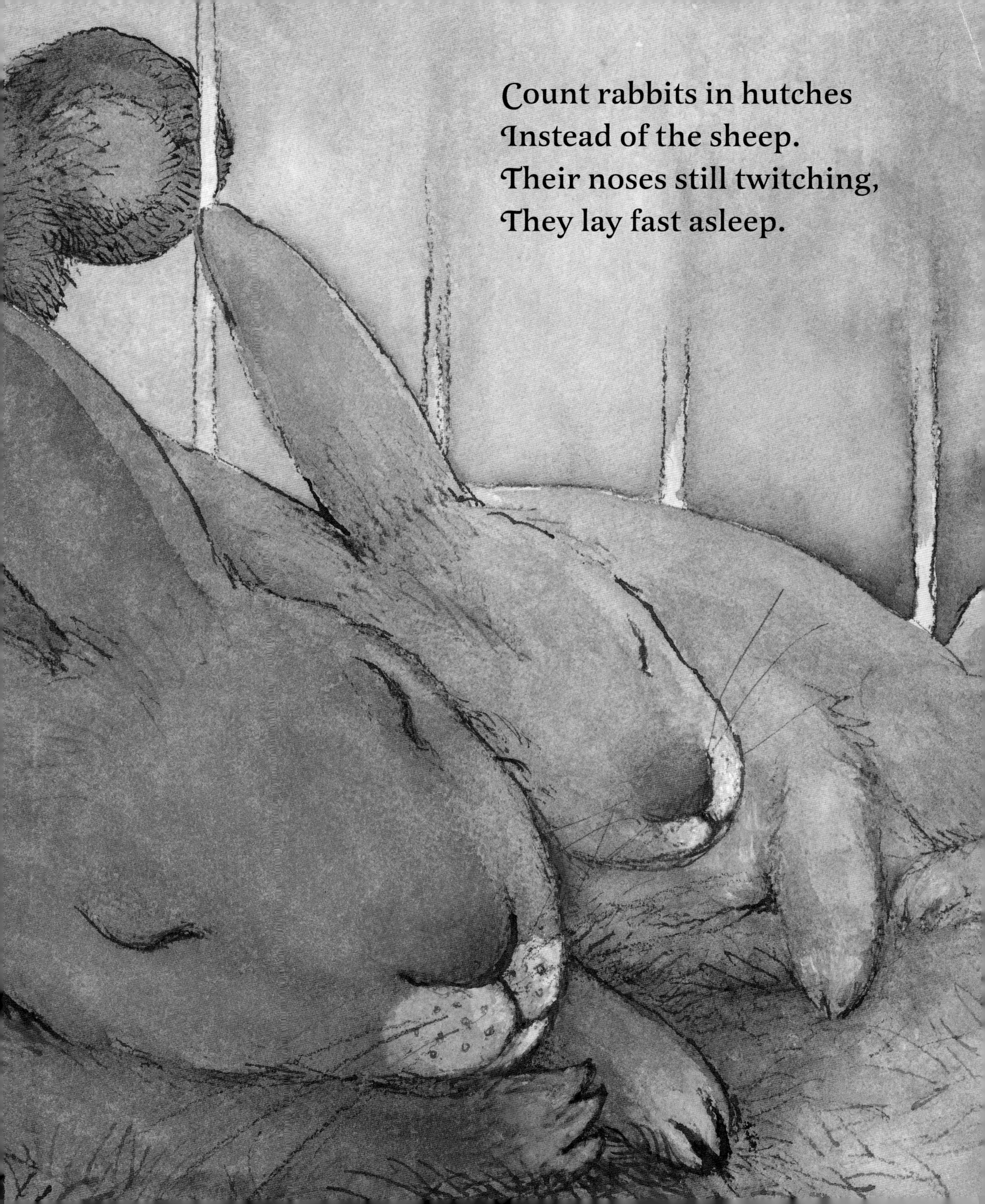

Count rabbits in hutches
Instead of the sheep.
Their noses still twitching,
They lay fast asleep.

With all of this counting
You feel like the sheep.
At last you are ready
To drift off to sleep!

For Daniel Lawrence Kleeger, with love
—L. N.
For Laura and Tamar, true believers
—D. M.

Editor: Tamar Brazis
Designer: Edward Miller
Production Manager: Alexis Mentor

Library of Congress Cataloging-in-Publication Data
Numeroff, Laura Joffe.
When sheep sleep / by Laura Numeroff ; illustrated by David McPhail.
p. cm.
Summary: Rhyming text suggests other options when one tries to count sheep but discovers that they are all asleep.
[1. Animals—Fiction. 2. Counting—Fiction. 3. Sleep—Fiction. 4. Bedtime—Fiction. 5. Stories in rhyme.] I. McPhail, David, 1940– ill. II. Title.

PZ8.3.N92Whe 2006
[E]—dc22
2005022544

ISBN 10: 0-8109-5469-9
ISBN 13: 978-0-8109-5469-4

Printed and bound in China
10 9 8 7 6 5 4 3 2 1

HNA
harry n. abrams, inc.
a subsidiary of La Martinière Groupe

115 West 18th Street
New York, NY 10011
www.hnabooks.com